**www.NaptimeAdventures.com**

*Come dream with us!*

*See other books in this series -- information inside back cover*

# The Big Ocean

## An Underwater Naptime Adventure ™

### Volume 2 of the Naptime Adventure ™ series

by D. R. Thompson
Illustrated by D. R. & Dave Thompson

SAN 254 783X
This New World Publishing, LLC
13500 SW Pacific Hwy, Suite 129
Tigard, OR 97223

www.ThisNewWorld.com

Printed in China

Thompson, D.R., 1963-
    The big ocean : an underwater naptime adventure/ by
D.R. Thompson ; illustrated with Dave Thompson ; design,
layout, and cover by Dave Thompson.
    p. cm -- (The naptime adventure series ; v. 2)
    SUMMARY: During a nap at the beach, a young girl
dreams that she and her mother explore the ocean as
mermaids. Or was it a dream?
    Audience: Ages 3-8.
    LCCN 2003116391
    ISBN 0-9723252-2-0


    1. Dreams--Juvenile fiction. 2. Ocean--Juvenile
fiction. 3. Mermaids--Juvenile fiction. [1. Dreams--
Fiction. 2. Ocean--Fiction. 3. Mermaids--Fiction.
4. Stories in rhyme.]   I. Thompson, Dave, 1963-   II.
Title.

PZ8.3.T3197Bi 2003          [E]
                   QBI33-1742

**www.NaptimeAdventures.com**
*Come dream with us.*

**Design, cover, and layout by:**
Dave Thompson

To everyone who loves the water.

As they sat on the beach, dad said it was true:

our world is mostly just oceans of blue.

"It's so big,"
said young Sally.
"The sea is so bare,
It goes on
forever,
just water
out there."

After making a sand castle they lay down for a nap,
underneath an umbrella, in the shade on a mat.

As they dozed off to sleep,
Sally woke with a start.
And she tried to get up,
but her legs would not part.

Then her legs started changing
their shape and their color.
They had scales, and she could not
tell one from the other.

As they floated down under, they watched the waves smash on the shore against rocks, making roars as they crashed.

An octopus, urchin, anemones, and rays --

they never knew life came in so many ways.

Then out beyond these, the low tide's cool pools,
through forests of kelp full of fishes in schools.

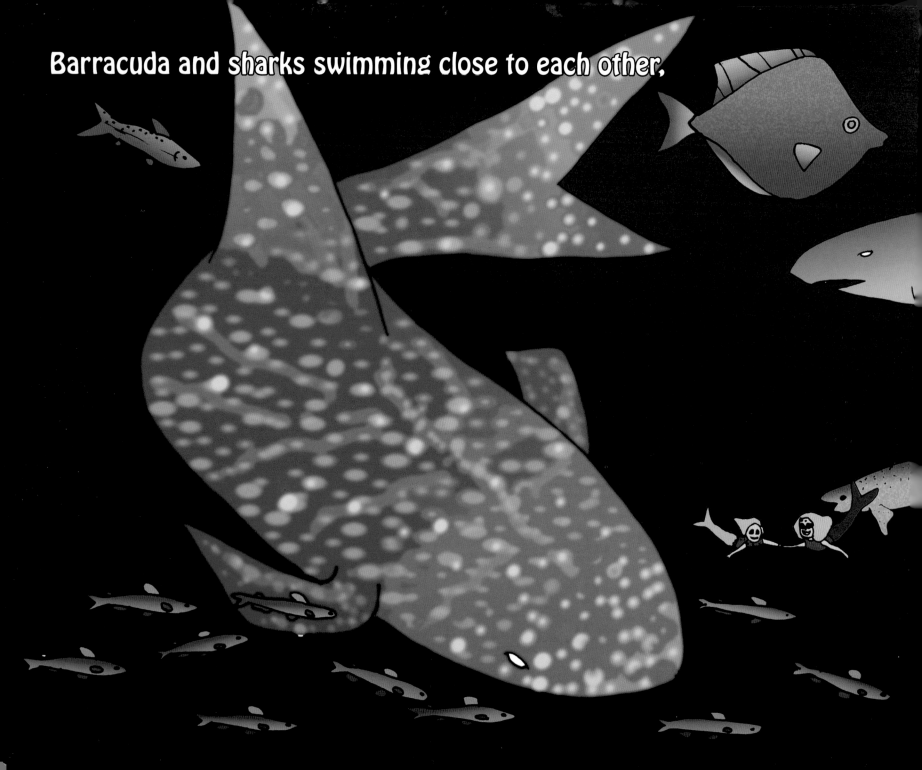

Barracuda and sharks swimming close to each other,

"Wow, it's crowded down here!" Sally said to her mother.

They were startled to see
all the colors of fish,

and the blizzard of jellyfish swirl and swish.

Then swimming along to an old sunken ship,

that was covered with life from the end to the tip!

Amazing! A sea cave
hidden under a ledge.
It was just a bit scary --
they stayed near the
edge.

"Let's head on home now, I'm ready to go."
The mom said OK, but how? She did not know.

Then they saw dolphins swimming after a ship, and in the distance, a lighthouse on a peninsula tip.

They swam back to the beach
where they'd started that day,

passing more and more kinds
of sea life on the way.

Then, pulling themselves from the rocks to the sand, their fins dragged behind them, not much use here on land.

Then, tired but happy,
they lay on their mat,
They weren't sure if they'd ever
had more fun than that!

And then...

When they woke, they had legs,
like you'd think they would.
She knew she'd been dreaming,
but Sally-Ann did feel good.

The ocean was big, the ocean was full.
With so much to see, the ocean was cool!

# The End!

More information? Turn the page.

# COMING SOON!

## MY BABY SISTER

### A FRIENDS-SOMEDAY NAPTIME ADVENTURE

A new baby sister has arrived, and Sally-Ann feels that the baby is too much work. During her naptime dream, her sister is now the same age as she is! Sally-Ann shows her "everything," and they play together all afternoon. Sally-Ann gains a new appreciation for who her sister will become, and is now content to wait for her little sister to grow up.

ISBN 0-9723252-3-9

Kids! Enter our contest to win cool prizes!

Rules and entry form on our Web site.

Plus, get free tips on how to write a story.

# Ordering Information:

The Naptime Adventure books are available at bookstores, online bookstores, and by calling 800-462-6420.

Or, send check or money order for $14.95 plus $4.00 shipping and handling within the United States ($9.00 shipping and handling outside of the United States) per book to:

This New World Publishing

13500 SW Pacific Highway, Suite 129-B

Tigard, OR  97223

USA

PLEASE SPECIFY THE TITLE OF THE BOOK YOU WOULD LIKE

**www.ThisNewWorld.com**

*Register for special offers and author workshops on-line!*